CONTENTS
• • • • • • • • • • • • • • •

SIR PORKY

Horsing Around in Camelot

by Tracey West

Illustrated by Duendes del Sur

SCHOLASTIC INC.

New York   Toronto   London   Auckland   Sydney
Mexico City   New Delhi   Hong Kong   Buenos Aires

for Yesmia Cueva

This book is a work of hysterical fiction. Any similarities to actual historical persons, places, or events are likely to be wacky. In other words: don't use this book for a history report!

Published by Scholastic Inc.,
90 Old Sherman Turnpike,
Danbury, Connecticut 06816.

0-439-56584-7

Printed in the U.S.A.
First printing, November 2003

It's T-T-T-Time-Travel Time Again

It's m-m-m-me, Porky Pig, here at the Warner Brothers Movie Studios. (That's WB Studio for short.) L-l-l-let me tell you, things haven't been the same around here since the ACME Space Replacer arrived.

The Space Replacer looks s-s-s-sort of like a soda machine with a computer keyboard and a big red button on one side and a long metal rod on the other. This gadget can take any of us to any place at any time. We can go back or forward in time, too. B-b-b-but that's not all—the Space Replacer has another part to it, the Re-replacer. It tells us interesting and h-h-helpful stuff about the place we've been zapped to. The Re-replacer also tells us where we have to be, called the checkpoint, and when we have to be there so that it can beam us home. Oh, and everybody who travels has to be there. If we don't all make it to that place in time, n-n-n-no one can return.

The other Looney Tunes characters and I

have time-traveled in the Space Replacer. You p-p-p-probably know some of my fellow time travelers. Here's who came with me on this, my latest time-travel adventure. There's Daffy Duck, he's a major talent—just ask him. Then there's Taz, which is short for Tasmanian Devil, who also came with us. He has a major talent, too— a talent for eating.

This time, Daffy and I used the Space Replacer to visit the legendary King Arthur. Along the way, we faced many dangers, not the least of which was a fierce dragon. And when we discovered that Taz had joined us, things really got wild. Keep reading to find out how I b-b-b-became knighted and how the famous Merlin helped us return to present-day.

Porky Pig

CHAPTER 1

Taz Hungry!

"Cut! That's a wrap, everybody!" the movie director shouted. "Have a great weekend."

It was another busy day of filming on the Warner Bros. lot. Crew members scurried around taking down lights and scenery. But Porky Pig, the star of the film, hadn't budged.

The round little pig wore a suit of armor, like a knight from days of old. He lifted up the face piece on his silver helmet. "D-d-d-do we have to stop now?" Porky asked. "I'm j-j-j-just getting warmed up!"

Granny was sitting on the sidelines, rocking in a rocking chair. The sweet old lady was knitting a sweater for her cat, Sylvester, while Tweety Bird sat on her shoulder. "My, you look handsome in that armor, Porky dear," Granny said admiringly.

"Aw, th-th-th-thanks, Granny," Porky replied, blushing. "Do you really think so?"

Granny nodded. "I'm sure you would have made a fine knight."

"I don't know," Porky said. "Knights are very brave, not like me. But I wish I could have met King Arthur. Wh-wh-wh-what a hero!"

Porky had read every book he could find about King Arthur. He loved the old tales of Arthur and his brave knights.

"You can meet King Arthur if you want to," Tweety piped up. "Just use the Space Replacer thingy."

The Space Replacer was a strange machine that had turned up on the WB lot one day. It could send them to any place or time they could imagine. Even to the time of King Arthur.

But using the Space Replacer could be dangerous. They never knew what would happen after they were transported.

"I d-d-don't know, Tweety," Porky said. "That's one funny machine!"

Porky said good-bye to Granny and Tweety. As he walked to his dressing room, he passed a door marked Stage 51. The Space Replacer was kept in Stage 51. It couldn't hurt to look, could it?

The door squeaked open, and Porky stepped inside. The room was crowded with boxes and crates. Right in the middle of the room stood the Space Replacer. It was a metal box the same size and shape as a soda machine. The Beam Activator, a long metal rod, stuck out from one side. The front of the Space Replacer had a big red button and a built-in computer keyboard.

Porky stepped closer to the machine. It would be so easy, and he'd done it before. All he

had to do was type in some words on the keyboard, press the big red button, and he'd be whisked away to King Arthur's kingdom.

The little pig looked down at his suit of armor. Somehow, just wearing it made him feel brave. If King Arthur's knights could be brave, then why couldn't he?

Porky took a deep breath. He opened a small door on the Space Replacer and took out something that looked like a wristwatch. Porky strapped the Re-replacer to his wrist. He knew that he couldn't return to the WB lot without it.

Then Porky typed some words into the keyboard: **KING ARTHUR'S CAMELOT**. He took another deep breath and turned the metal rod so that it was pointed right at him. Then Porky lowered the face piece on his helmet. "King Arthur, h-h-h-here I come!" Porky cried. He pressed the red button. Instantly a laser beam shot out from the Beam Activator.

Zap! The beam hit Porky, and he vanished.

Meanwhile, Taz was banging on the door of the cafeteria. The Tasmanian Devil's stomach growled. He wanted food. Now! But the doors would not open. He pounded and pounded and pounded on the door.

At the same time, Daffy Duck came storming by the cafeteria. "Whoever heard of a pudgy pig playing a knight?" he fumed. "They should have given me that role. *They're despicable!* All of them."

Daffy was too steamed to see where he was going. He bumped right into Taz. "Watch where you're going, you fur ball!" Daffy snapped.

Taz's blood began to boil. The duck had bumped him. Taz didn't like that. Taz was hungry. Taz wanted food. Then an idea popped into Taz's head. Duck was food. Duck was *good* food. *"Gababababarrrrrrrgh!"* Taz growled. Then he charged after Daffy.

"Hey, I was just kidding!" Daffy sputtered. "There's nothing wrong with being furry."

Daffy ran as fast as his webbed feet would go. He could feel Taz's hot breath right on his tail feathers. He had to hide—and quick! Then he saw an open door up ahead. Daffy ran inside and slammed it behind him. He pushed a stack of boxes against the door.

"Grrrrababararala!" Taz fumed, banging on the door.

Daffy looked around. There was no way to escape.

Then he spied the Space Replacer.

Taz banged, and the door hinges creaked against his weight. It was only a matter of time. Daffy had no choice. He ran to the Space Replacer,

stood under the Beam Activator, and pressed the big red button.

"*BRAALARARAARARA!*" Taz burst through the door at the same moment. He lunged at Daffy just as the laser beam hit him.

Zap!

In the next instant, Stage 51 was perfectly quiet.

Both Daffy *and* Taz had disappeared!

CHAPTER 2
Porky the Hero

Porky Pig felt like he was falling from the sky. ***Thud!*** He landed on something hard. He lifted his knight's helmet and looked down. He was sitting on something green and tough. And it was moving!

Porky had landed on the back of a huge beast. It had broad shoulders and a long, curved tail. Sharp spines ran down its back, and fire blasted from its mouth. ***"A d-d-dra-dragon!"*** Porky yelled.

The dragon turned its head and saw Porky on

its back. **"Raaaaaaaawr!"** It ran in circles, like a dog chasing its tail. Porky grabbed onto a spine and held on with all his might.

The dragon stumbled and fell. **Splash!** Cold water hit Porky's face. The dragon had fallen into a small lake. The beast let out another angry roar. It stood up and shook the water off its back. Porky's armor clanked as he swung from side to side.

Just then he noticed a group of men in knight's armor standing along the shore. They were shouting and waving swords. The dragon noticed them, too. It reared back its head, ready to blast them with fire. "Oh, g-g-g-goodness!" Porky wailed. He closed his eyes. He just couldn't watch.

"Aaaaaaaaaaaa-choo!"

Achoo? Porky opened his eyes. The lake water had doused the dragon's flames. All the dragon could do was sneeze!

"Serves you right, you terrible beast!" one of the knights yelled.

The dragon made a whimpering noise, like a small puppy. Then it swiftly turned and started to run. Porky lost his grip and tumbled into the water. He felt himself sinking fast. His heavy armor dragged him down. He waved his arms, but he couldn't stay afloat.

Suddenly a long stick appeared above Porky's head. It looked like a jousting pole, a kind of weapon knights used when fighting on horseback. Porky grabbed it and was quickly lifted into the air. Finally, his feet hit solid ground.

He was surrounded by knights—real, live knights! He had landed in King Arthur's Camelot after all.

One of the knights took off his helmet. He was a big man with a bushy, blond beard. "Good sir," he said. "You have bravely fought the dragon. We owe you our thanks."

"B-b-b-brave? Me?" Porky asked.

"Aye," said the knight. "As brave as any knight in King Arthur's court. If you allow us, we will take you there now and feast in your honor. But first, can you tell us your name? You are a mystery to us."

Porky took off his helmet. "I'm Porky P-P-Pig!" he said.

The knight bowed. "And I am Sir Kay," he said. "You are a strange fellow, to be sure, Porky Pig. Our king will surely want to meet you."

The knights mounted their horses. Sir Kay lifted Porky onto the back of a tall white horse. Then he jumped on in front of Porky. "To the castle!" Sir Kay cried.

The other knights let out a rousing cheer. Sir Kay kicked his horse's flanks, and the horse took off.

"Whoa!" Porky cried. He grabbed onto the saddle. Riding the horse was easier than riding the dragon—but not much.

As they galloped away, Porky couldn't believe he had done it. Was he really in King Arthur's Camelot? There was only one way to be sure. He pushed the black button on the Re-replacer he wore around his wrist. Important information popped up:

> **WHERE:** King Arthur's kingdom of Camelot
> **WHEN:** long ago
> **WHO:** 3 travelers, 2 missing
> **TIME REMAINING:** 16 hours, 36 minutes
> **RETURN CHECKPOINT:** the Enchanted Oak

Porky knew there were certain rules when using the Re-replacer. To get back home, he had to be at the return checkpoint. This time, it was something called the Enchanted Oak.

"I'm sure someone in King Arthur's court can tell me where that is," Porky thought confidently.

He also had to be at the checkpoint at an exact time. Porky had 16 hours and 36 minutes to get there.

"P-p-p-perfect!" Porky thought. "I can spend the night here!"

There was one more rule. *Everyone* who had traveled to a place had to be at the checkpoint. If all the travelers weren't there, nobody could go home.

Porky frowned. According to the Re-replacer, three travelers had come to King Arthur's time, not one. But that didn't make sense. Only Porky had used the Space Replacer. It had to be some kind of mistake.

Didn't it?

CHAPTER 3

Presenting . . . Sir Porky!

After an hour of bumping along, Sir Kay's horse came to a stop. The knight stepped down from his horse. "We are here, Porky Pig," he said. "Welcome to Camelot!"

Porky gasped. A tall castle made of white stone gleamed in the sunlight. Round towers rose up so high that some of them seemed to touch the clouds. From each tower waved a white flag with a red dragon on it. Porky knew this was the symbol of King Arthur himself.

Porky couldn't believe he was really in Camelot. To be sure, he pressed the white button on his Re-replacer. The little screen revealed all kinds of facts about people, places, and things. The message said:

Camelot

No, it's not a place with a lot of camels. According to legend, Camelot was the central city of King Arthur's kingdom.

"*Oh, b-b-b-boy!*" Porky cried. "I'm really here!"

Sir Kay lifted Porky off the horse and placed him on the ground. "First, we will clean up," the knight said. "And then you shall meet our king."

Porky could hardly wait. He followed Sir Kay and the knights across a wooden bridge. The bridge crossed a moat that made a circle around the castle. Porky looked down into the dark, bubbling water. He shivered. Who knew what strange creatures lurked there?

The knights and Porky walked into a large hallway. Sir Kay clapped his hands. **"Squire!"** he called out.

A young boy came running and stopped in front of Sir Kay. "This brave stranger has defeated the dragon," Sir Kay said. "Please see that he has clean clothes. Then we will take him to the king."

The boy looked at Porky, and his eyes widened. The squire was about half the size of Sir Kay, and Porky was about half the size of the squire. He thought that Porky was a strange fellow, indeed.

The squire nodded, turned to Porky, and bowed. "Follow me," he said. He led Porky to a small, cozy room. The room held a straw-stuffed mattress, a wooden table, and a large jug of water. A fire burned in a small fireplace.

"I'll be back with some clothes as fast as I can, sir," the boy said. He returned a few moments later with a white shirt, a small pair of black boots, and green puffy pants.

"Th-th-th-thanks!" Porky said. "I'm Porky Pig. What's your name?"

"They call me Red, sir," the boy said, pointing to his messy mop of red hair. "I am pleased to be in your service."

"Sir Kay called you s-s-s-squire," Porky said. "That means you're training to become a knight some day, doesn't it?"

Red nodded. "It would be a great honor to serve the king."

"K-K-K-King Arthur himself!" Porky said, beaming. "I can't wait to meet him."

"Then let's get you dressed, sir," Red said. Porky slipped out of the armor that was his costume on the WB lot. Red helped him into his clothes. He even made room for Porky's curly tail to stick out in back.

"G-g-g-great!" Porky said proudly. **"Let's g-g-g-go!"**

Red led Porky through the castle to a large round room. Almost every inch of space was taken up by a huge round table in the center. Knights were seated all around the table. "There must be a h-h-h-hundred of them!" Porky gasped.

Two high-backed chairs rose from one side of the circle. A beautiful woman in a pale blue dress sat in one chair. A silver crown sat atop her brown curls. Next to her sat a man wearing a red robe and a gold crown.

"Is th-th-th-that him?" Porky whispered.

Red nodded. "That is King Arthur, and she is Queen Guinevere."

King Arthur spotted Porky and rose to his feet. "Sir Kay!" he called out. "Is this the brave stranger I have heard so much about?"

Sir Kay rose from his place at the table. "Indeed it is, sire. May I present Porky Pig."

Porky couldn't move. He couldn't believe it. He was really meeting King Arthur! It was like a dream come true. Then he heard Red hiss

in his ear. **"Bow, Porky!"**

"Of c-c-c-course," Porky said, blushing. He bowed toward the king. Then he felt Red give him a little push. Porky walked around the circle until he reached King Arthur. Then he bowed again. "It is a pleasure to meet you, K-K-K-King Arthur," he said.

"Is it true that you rode the dragon?" King Arthur asked.

"S-s-s-sort of," Porky said, blushing again. "It was really kind of an accident."

"Such modesty!" King Arthur bellowed. "I could use a brave knight like you in my service.

Tell me, do you serve another king?"

Porky shook his head. "N-n-n-no. You're my most favorite king who ever lived!"

"Then kneel, Porky Pig!" King Arthur cried. He took a sword from his side. Then he tapped the sword on Porky's head and on each of his shoulders. "I hereby dub you Sir Porky of the Round Table!" the king said. "You are now one of my knights."

The knights around the table cheered. Porky's cheeks turned bright red. "G-g-g-gosh," he said. "I don't know what to say."

"Say you will help us, Sir Porky!" All eyes in the room turned at the sound of the strange voice. A tall man with a long white beard entered the room. He wore a deep blue robe decorated with moons and stars.

"What news do you bring us, Merlin?" King Arthur asked.

Porky gasped. Was it really Merlin, the great wizard? He pressed the white button on the Re-replacer to be sure:

Merlin

This wizard was King Arthur's most trusted adviser. Some say that he possessed strange and mysterious powers. Others say that he possessed a strange and mysterious smell.

Knowing wizards, both stories are probably true.

Merlin approached the king. "I am afraid I have bad news, sire," the wizard said. "There are reports of a terrible creature loose in Camelot. It is a beast like no other. It is destroying the villages."

King Arthur frowned. But before he could

speak, another knight entered the room. The room went silent. The knight dragged in a horrible, slimy creature. Porky had never seen anything like it. Angry eyes bulged from its face. Mud and slime dripped from its body. "Look what I found sneaking around the moat!" said the knight.

Daffy Cleans Up His Act?

"Is th-th-th-that the horrible creature?" Porky asked nervously.

The creature struggled to free itself from the knight. "It's me, Daffy Duck, you idiot!" Daffy shook his head and some of the mud flew off.

Porky could see Daffy's orange beak.

"*D-D-D-Daffy!* It *is* you," Porky said.

"Do you know this beast, Sir Porky?" King Arthur asked.

Porky nodded. "He's my f-f-f-friend."

"Whatever you say, Porky," Daffy said. "Just tell Sir Grabs-a-lot here to let me go!"

The knight sniffed. "That's Sir Lancelot, thank you!"

King Arthur nodded. "Unhand him," he said. "Any friend of Sir Porky's is a friend of this court." Sir Lancelot let go of Daffy. The muddy duck stomped toward Porky.

"What kind of place is this?" he fumed. "I pressed the button on the Space Replacer to get away from Taz, and the next thing I know, I'm swimming around in a slimy moat!"

"It's s-s-s-so exciting, Daffy," Porky said. "We're in Camelot."

"Camelot? I don't see any camels," Daffy said.

Porky sighed. "I mean the legendary k-k-k-kingdom of Camelot. That's King Arthur and his knights."

"Well, that's just perfect!" Daffy complained. "The Dark Ages! I guess I can forget about getting a hot shower then, right?"

Porky was horrified. Didn't Daffy know he was insulting a powerful king? But King Arthur just laughed. "I fear your friend has had a hard trip," he said. "Merlin, see if you can help him."

Merlin bowed to the king. Then he took a long wand out from the folds of his robe. The wand looked like an ordinary wooden stick. Merlin pointed the wand at Daffy. He chanted some words under his breath. Then a shower of sparks flew from the wand.

Poof! The next instant Daffy was perfectly clean and dry!

"W-w-w-wonder—cool!" Porky cried.

Daffy smoothed out his feathers. "Now that's more like it," he said. "Can you make me a cheeseburger with that thing?"

Merlin frowned, puzzled.

"My friend means to say th-th-th-thank you," Porky said. Porky nudged Daffy and whispered, "Come on, let's sit down." Porky and Daffy took their places at the Round Table. As King Arthur and Merlin huddled together and talked in whispers, Porky decided to check the Re-Replacer:

WHERE: King Arthur's kingdom of Camelot
WHEN: long ago
WHO: 3 travelers, 1 missing
TIME REMAINING: 13 hours, 53 minutes
RETURN CHECKPOINT: the Enchanted Oak

Now he knew that Daffy was one of the three travelers. But who was the third? Then Porky remembered that Daffy said he had pressed the button on the Space Replacer to get away from Taz. Could Taz be the third traveler? Just thinking about it made Porky shiver. That hungry Tasmanian Devil was always trying to turn Porky into a pork chop.

Sitting beside him, Daffy was lost in thought, too. But he wasn't thinking about Taz. Daffy was thinking about Merlin's wand. "Just imagine what I could do with a gizmo like that!" Daffy thought. "*Poof!* A huge mansion. *Poof!* A brand new car."

King Arthur's voice boomed through the room. "I have made a decision," he said. "We must go to the village to see if these reports are

true. Sir Porky, I hope you will come with us. We could use a brave knight like you."

Daffy pointed at Porky. "Him?" he asked, shocked. "He's afraid of his own shadow!"

Porky looked down at his plate. Daffy was right. Landing on the dragon was just an accident. He wasn't really brave.

"We're counting on you, Sir Porky," Sir Kay called out.

Porky gulped. He had come to Camelot for an adventure. He couldn't back down now. "C-c-c-count me in!" he said.

"Your friend is welcome to come, too," King Arthur said.

"No, thanks," Daffy said. "I'll leave the monster hunting to the professionals." Then, chuckling to himself, Daffy thought, "And while the knights are out of the castle, I'll be free to swipe that wizard's wand."

CHAPTER 5

Taz on the Loose!

Porky changed into his armor and followed the knights out to the stables. Red brought out a small pony for Porky to ride. "I hope you don't mind," Red said. "I just thought old Spots here would be more to your liking."

"It's p-p-p-perfect!" Porky replied. He jumped on the pony's back. Spots turned his head to look at Porky. He raised an eyebrow, shook his head, and then plodded on after the rest of the knights.

Porky beamed with pride as he and the knights rode to the castle gates. King Arthur waited there for them on a beautiful white horse. *"To the village!"* the king cried.

The knights cheered and galloped across the bridge. Porky bounced along on his pony. *"W-w-w-wait for me!"* he yelled.

The nearest village was not far from the castle. Porky could see the small brown huts in the distance. But as he got closer, he saw that every hut had a hole ripped into its wall. Clothes, baskets, twigs, and apple cores littered the ground. It looked like a tornado had passed through. Men, women, and children walked through the rubble. They looked dazed. The villagers ran up to the knights as soon as they saw them. They all began to talk at once.

"It was terrible!"

"A hairy, drooling beast!"

"The monster ate everything in sight!"

Sir Kay climbed off his horse. "One at a time, please!" he yelled.

An old woman stepped to the front of the group. "I've lived a long time, and I've never seen a monster like this," she said. "It swept through the town so fast we could barely see it.

It ate all of the apples and all of the potatoes! And then it went after the sheep!"

Porky had a strange feeling that he knew who the monster was. He climbed off Spots and walked to one of the huts. Just as he thought. The hole in the hut was not a round hole at all. Porky aimed the Re-replacer at the hole and pressed the white button:

Taz Holes

Hole dimensions indicate the size and shape of one Tasmanian Devil.

If I were you, I'd get away from there quick!

It was true! Taz had followed Daffy into the Space Replacer and traveled to King Arthur's time. And Taz was hungry.

"I kn-kn-kn-know who this is!" Porky announced.

Sir Lancelot frowned. "Another friend of yours?" he asked.

"N-n-n-not exactly," Porky said.

King Arthur rode up between them. "Sir Porky knew how to ride a dragon," the king announced. "I am not surprised that he knows about this monster."

"Then Sir Porky shall be our leader," Sir Kay said. "He will lead us to the monster!"

Porky gulped. How could he lead King Arthur's knights?

King Arthur looked at the sky. "It will be dark soon. Porky and the knights will start out in the morning."

"Oh, d-d-d-dear!" Porky wailed inside his head, as they all headed back to the castle.

Daffy's Magic Moment

Later that night, Porky tossed and turned in his bed. Every time he closed his eyes, he saw Taz's huge, hungry mouth in his dreams.

Daffy Duck wasn't sleeping, either. But he wasn't thinking about Taz. He had other things on his mind. "I'll get my hands on that wand if it's the last thing I do!" Daffy promised himself.

When Porky and the knights rode to the village, Merlin had stayed behind. Daffy followed the wizard all around the castle. But Merlin never once put down the wand. "That wizard has to sleep some time. I'll wait until dark and grab the wand then," Daffy muttered.

Later on, Daffy crept through the castle halls to Merlin's room. Candles on the walls cast spooky shadows on the stone floor. Daffy came to a door marked with a carving of a moon.

It was Merlin's room. Daffy opened the door ever so slowly and tiptoed inside.

The light of the full moon shone through the window. Books filled the shelves that lined the walls. Merlin, snoring softly, slept in his bed underneath the window. A long wooden table sat in the center of the room. Bottles, feathers, rocks, and other strange items cluttered the top of the table.

And there, among the clutter, was the wand.

"Soon I'll be the most powerful duck in all of Hollywood!" Daffy whispered, rubbing his hands together. Step by step, Daffy tiptoed to the table. Slowly, he reached out to grab the wand.

He almost had it—but the wand began to roll. It rolled all the way down the table to the other end. *"Drat!"* Daffy muttered. The wizard was snoring loudly now. Daffy still had a chance. Step by step, he tiptoed to the end of the table. Slowly, he reached out to grab the wand.

But the wand rolled off the table. It continued across the floor and came to a stop in front of a bookcase. "I've got you now," Daffy whispered. He scurried to the bookcase and bent down to grab the wand.

Boink!

A book dropped on Daffy's head. ***"Ouch!"*** he wailed.

Boink! Boink! Boink!

The books seemed to be jumping off the shelves as they landed on Daffy's head. Soon the little black duck was buried under a pile of books.

"This is not funny!" Daffy complained, brushing the books aside. He put a hand over his beak. Had Merlin heard him? No, the wizard was still snoring away. Daffy felt something move under his webbed feet. He looked down to see the wand roll away. It rolled across the floor and right out the door.

Daffy chased after the wand. It rolled down the hall and bumped into an old suit of armor. Daffy dove after the wand . . .

Boink!

The armor helmet fell right on Daffy's head! "Who turned out the lights?" Daffy cried. The helmet was so heavy! Daffy wobbled around as he tried to pull it off.

Finally, with a mighty push, Daffy removed the helmet. The wand was standing straight up in front of Daffy. He shook his fist at the wand. "I'll turn you into firewood, you slippery stick!"

Zap!

A flash of light burst from the wand, and Daffy's body tingled. Whiskers stuck out of his face, and he had little clawed feet instead of webbed ones. All of a sudden he wanted cheese . . .

The wand had turned him into a mouse!

"Turn me back right now!" Daffy squeaked.

Zap!

The wand flashed, and Daffy's body tingled again. He looked down. His webbed feet were back . . . but they were green. And instead of cheese, he was hungry for fat, juicy flies.

The wand had turned him into a frog! "All right, all right," Daffy croaked. "Forget what I said about the firewood. Just turn me back!"

Zap!

Daffy transformed again. He felt bigger, somehow. He wiggled his behind and discovered he had a tail again. "Thanks!" Daffy said.

Then he caught his reflection in the shiny armor. A dragon stared back at him. A dragon with black scales and an orange snout. **"Help!"** Daffy yelled.

At the sound of Daffy's cry, the knights ran
out of their rooms. They wore sleeping gowns,
but they all carried their swords. *"A dragon!"*
Sir Kay cried. *"Let us slay him!"*

The knights charged after Daffy. He ran
through the halls of the castle, dragging his
dragon tail behind him. He turned a corner . . .
and ran right into a dead end. There was
nowhere to run. He turned to face the angry
knights. "Don't come near me!" he yelled.
"I'll . . . I'll blast you with my fiery breath!"

Daffy took a deep breath. Then he blew as hard as he could.

Poof!

A tiny puff of smoke came out. It floated toward Sir Kay, but the knight brushed it away. **"Die, dragon!"** he cried.

Daffy closed his eyes as the knights charged at him. Then he heard a familiar voice. "W-w-w-wait for me, guys!" Porky came running down the hall, waving a small dagger.

"Porky! **It's me!**" Daffy yelled. "Your old pal, Daffy Duck!"

Sir Kay motioned for the knights to stop. "Is this true, Porky Pig?" he asked.

Porky squinted at Daffy. "I d-d-d-don't know," he said. "He sure looks like a dragon to m-m-m-me."

Then Porky remembered the Re-replacer. He pressed the white button and read:

Big Ugly Thing
What are you asking me for? I've never seen anything like it.

Daffy stomped a dragon foot. "You stuttering simpleton! You dolt! It's me, Daffy Duck, you brainless bumpkin!"

Porky smiled. "That's D-D-D-Daf—that's him, all right. Don't hurt him, fellas."

Merlin pushed through the small crowd. He held his wand in one hand. "What has happened here?" Merlin asked. Then he got a look at Daffy and frowned.

He turned to his wand. "Did you do this?" he asked. The wand turned away from him, avoiding Merlin's questioning stare.

Merlin shook his head. "You can all go back to sleep," he said. "I can take care of this."

"You're lucky I held back my fiery breath on purpose!" Daffy called out as the knights returned to their rooms. "I could have turned you into french fries if I wanted to!"

CHAPTER 8

Merlin's Potions

"It's not my fault! That wacky wand of yours attacked me for no reason!" Daffy complained. He was still stuck in his dragon form. He slumped on the floor in Merlin's room.

Porky Pig watched as Merlin fussed with bottles of potions on his worktable. The wizard had lit some candles to light up the room. He frowned as he studied the bottles.

"I'm not sure what kind of magic my wand used on Daffy," Merlin said. "But I'll figure it out. You'll be back to normal soon—if you can call that normal." The wizard muffled the last few words.

"I heard that!" Daffy snapped.

Porky looked out the window. The sky was growing lighter. He checked the Re-replacer for the latest information:

> **WHERE:** King Arthur's kingdom of Camelot
> **WHEN:** long ago
> **WHO:** 3 travelers, 1 missing
> **TIME REMAINING:** 7 hours, 12 minutes
> **RETURN CHECKPOINT:** the Enchanted Oak

"Oh, d-d-d-dear," Porky said. They only had 7 hours left. Not much time to find Taz and get to the Enchanted Oak, or they'd be stuck in Camelot forever.

King Arthur was nice. So were the knights. But the magic, monsters, and dragons were getting to be too much for Porky. At home, everything was safe.

"What is the matter?" Merlin asked.

"It's a l-l-l-long story," Porky said. "You see, M-M-M-Merlin, we're not from around here."

Merlin smiled. "I knew that, Sir Porky. I have seen many strange things in my time, but you and your friend are special. I would like to hear your story."

Daffy jumped to his feet. "Hey! What about me? I'm still a dragon, remember?"

Merlin ignored him. "Go on, Sir Porky," he said, stirring a potion.

So Porky told Merlin all about the Space Replacer. He explained that the monster scaring the villagers was Taz. "We have to find Taz, and g-g-g-get to the Enchanted Oak in 7 hours," Porky said. "Or we'll be stuck here forever."

Merlin nodded. "I can take you to the Enchanted Oak. Finding this Taz creature is another matter."

Porky felt better talking to Merlin. He watched as the wizard poured a bottle of blue liquid into a bottle of red liquid. A puff of smoke shot out of the bottle. Inside was a sparkling purple potion.

Merlin turned to Daffy. "Open your mouth

and say, 'aaaaah,' " he said.

Daffy frowned. "Are you crazy? I'm not drinking that stuff. What do you think I— gulp!" Merlin had poured the bottle into Daffy's open mouth.

Boom!

Daffy the dragon exploded in a cloud of smoke. When the smoke cleared, Daffy stood there, a regular duck again. "It's about time!" Daffy complained.

"Daffy!" Porky scolded. "You could say th-th-th-thank you."

"Thanks for nothing!" Daffy sputtered. "I wouldn't be in this mess if it wasn't for that wand. It attacked me, I tell you!"

Porky thought he heard the wand give a little growl from its place on the table. "That was an amazing p-p-p-potion!" Porky told Merlin.

The wizard smiled. "I have many potions, Sir Porky. Love potions, wealth potions, sleeping potions . . . "

"S-s-s-sleeping potions?" Porky asked.

"That's right," Merlin said. "Why, you could put a dragon to sleep with just a few drops!"

"Hmm," Porky muttered. A sleeping potion just might be the answer to their problem. *"I think I have a p-p-p-plan!"* the clever little pig said thoughtfully.

CHAPTER 9

A Pig, a Plan, and a Sheep

The next morning, Porky rode across the castle bridge on Spots. Behind him rode King Arthur and his knights.

"Sir Porky shall lead us to the monster!" Sir Kay cried. The knights let out a cheer.

Merlin rode up to Porky's side. His gray horse pulled a small cart behind him. A heavy sack hung from the horse's saddle. "I h-h-h-hope our plan works!" Porky said nervously.

"The plan is a good one," Merlin said. "The stars are in our favor, Sir Porky."

The heavy sack began to wiggle. Then Daffy Duck's head popped out of the sack. "What kind of star treatment is this?" Daffy wailed. "When my agent hears about this—"

"Wh-wh-wh-what are you doing in there, Daffy?" Porky asked.

"Ask your wizard friend," Daffy pouted.

"I'd just like to keep an eye on you," Merlin said. "We can't afford any trouble today."

"This is ridiculous!" Daffy sputtered. "I demand to see a lawyer!"

Merlin stuffed Daffy's head back in the sack and smiled. *"Onward!"* the wizard cried.

The knights charged into the village. The villagers cheered when they saw the knights.

"Have you come to slay the monster?" a little boy asked Porky.

"H-h-hope-hopeful—sort of," Porky said. "We have a p-p-p-plan!"

Porky climbed off Spots and walked to the wagon. A blanket covered something large and bulky. Porky pulled it off. *"T-t-t-ta da!"* he sang out.

The villagers scratched their heads. The knights scratched their helmets.

Sitting on the wagon was a sheep—at least, it

looked like a sheep. Porky and Merlin had made it the night before out of wood and cloth.

Sir Kay climbed off his horse and approached Porky. "Forgive me, Sir Porky," he said. "But how will this help us catch the monster?"

"It's easy," Porky said. "It's stuffed with a s-s-s-sleeping potion! When Taz eats it, he'll fall asleep. Then Daffy and I will take him away from Camelot."

"*Taz?*" asked Sir Kay.

"Th-th-th-that's the name of the monster," Porky said.

The knights unloaded the sheep from the

wagon and carried it to a nearby field. Then they all crouched behind some bushes. Merlin kept Daffy close by his side.

Then they waited.

Minutes passed, but nothing happened.

Porky frowned. Then he had an idea. **"Baaaaaa! Baaaaaa!"** Porky made a noise like a sheep.

"Good thinking, Sir Porky!" Merlin said.

Porky kept baaaa-ing. Daffy squirmed in his sack. "I've got to get out of here before that hungry hair ball Taz shows up," he said. But how would he get out of the sack? The ropes tied around the top were just too tight. Then he noticed Spots munching on some grass. Daffy wriggled across the ground until he came to the pony. "Nice horsey," he said. "How would you like to eat some nice, tasty rope? It's much better than grass."

Spots plodded over and began chewing on the ropes. Soon Daffy was free!

"Sorry, Porky!" Daffy said, pulling the Re-replacer off Porky's wrist. "But it's time for me to scram. Tell Taz I said hello."

"D-D-D-Daffy, wait!" Porky yelled.

But Daffy darted through the knights and ran

through the village . . .

. . . and right into **Taz!**

"Mmm. Drabagraba!" Taz said. He picked up Daffy and threw him over his shoulder.

The knights stared, frozen. They had never seen a monster like Taz before.

"It s-s-s-serves Daffy right," Porky thought. "I should just let Taz eat him for lunch!" Then Porky remembered that Daffy had the Re-replacer. Porky sighed. If he didn't save Daffy, none of them would ever get home.

But was Porky brave enough to save Daffy? There was only one way to find out. Porky held out his dagger. **"S-s-s-stop**, in the name of King Arthur!" Porky yelled. Then he charged at Taz.

CHAPTER 10

One Enchanted Ending

Porky bounced around Taz, waving his sword and yelling.

The Tasmanian Devil looked confused. He had never eaten food that danced before. He sighed, then picked up Porky and threw him over his other shoulder.

"H-h-h-help!" Porky cried.

"I hate to say I told you so, Porky," Daffy said, "but I told you so!"

Suddenly there was a flash of light. In the

next instant Porky found himself back with the knights, safe. So was Daffy. Taz suddenly had the fake sheep slung over his shoulder. Porky looked at Merlin. The wizard pointed to his wand and smiled. Merlin had used his magic to switch Porky and Daffy for the sheep!

Taz didn't seem to mind. He drooled and licked his lips. He opened his huge mouth and stuffed the sheep inside. Then he gulped it down.

No one spoke. Would the plan work?

"Grababaragararg-zzzzzzzzzzzzzzz," Taz dropped to the ground and began to snore.

The knights let out a rousing cheer.

"It worked!" King Arthur cried. "Three cheers for Sir Porky!"

Sir Kay hoisted Porky on his shoulders. "Hip, hip, hooray!" the knights yelled.

"Hey, what about me?" Daffy complained. "I'm the one who got Taz to come here, remember?"

Porky had never felt happier. He had fought with King Arthur's knights. He couldn't wait to tell everyone back at the WB Studio.

"Oh n-n-n-no!" Porky wailed. He had forgotten all about the time. He quickly checked the Re-replacer:

WHERE: King Arthur's kingdom of Camelot
WHEN: long ago
WHO: 3 travelers
TIME REMAINING: 3 minutes
RETURN CHECKPOINT: the Enchanted Oak

"What's wrong, Sir Porky?" Merlin asked.

"We have to get to the Enchanted Oak in a few m-m-m-minutes, or we can't g-g-g-go home," he cried.

Merlin tapped his wand. "No problem, Sir Porky. My wand can get you there. But we'll miss you."

"I'll m-m-m-miss you, too," Porky said.

Porky said good-bye to King Arthur, Sir Kay, and the knights. He patted Spots on the head. "Good-bye, b-b-b-buddy," he said.

"Now go stand by Taz, and I'll transport you all together," Merlin said.

"Oh no!" Daffy yelled. "I'm not going near that beast."

Merlin pointed his wand at Daffy. "Would you rather become a dragon?"

Daffy sighed and stomped up to Porky and

the sleeping Taz.

Merlin waved his wand.

"Th-th-th-that's all, folks!" Porky called out.

Porky, Daffy, and Taz instantly vanished. They reappeared next to a huge old oak tree. "The Enchanted Oak!" Porky cried.

They were just in time. A ball of light shot out of the Re-replacer. *Zap!*

The next thing they knew, they were back at Stage 51, next to the Space Replacer. Porky and Daffy looked at Taz.

"Wh-wh-wh-what should we do with him?" Porky asked.

"Let's beam him into outer space," Daffy suggested, fiddling with the controls of the Space Replacer.

"I've got a b-b-bet—another idea," Porky said.

Porky and Daffy dragged Taz into the cafeteria. They were just in time. As soon as he woke up, Taz started eating all of the food in sight.

"That was f-f-f-fun, wasn't it?" Porky asked Daffy.

"Speak for yourself," Daffy complained. "I'm never going near that Space Replacer again. I mean it this time!"

Porky just smiled. He would never forget his adventure with King Arthur.

"See ya, Porky," Daffy said as he headed out the door.

"That's
S-S-S-Sir
Porky to you!"
Porky reminded him.